THE BROKEN WINDOW

Jonathan Newman

ISBN: 9798537596035

For Lily and Joshua

Many thanks to:
- the "Austro-Monks": Tho Bishop, Tate Fegley, Kristoffer Hansen, Karras Lambert, Ash Navabi, and George Pickering.
- the Mises Institute, for introducing me to the works of great economists like Bastiat and Hazlitt.
- my wonderful wife, Lauren.

That Paul is a hoodlum. He's MEAN and destructive.

But one of his misdeeds became quite instructive.

He picked up a brick and then wound up his arm.

He aimed at a WINDOW to cause the most harm.

BAKERY
OPEN

The bakery window was shattered in pieces.

A crowd gathers 'round as the tension increases.

"Oh, what shall we say of this terrible act?"

Asked the man in the front,

The window is broken.
Yes, that much is true.
The baker's misfortune
is easy to view.

And that's how the story of this crime was **SPUN**.

"The baker will pay for the glazier to mend it."

"The money moves on 'cause the glazier will **SPEND** it."

The crowd all agreed that destruction is fine.

New jobs and new spending mean no one should whine.

HENRY and FRED'RIC show up on the scene

to let the crowd know they forgot the UNSEEN.

They thought of the jobs and the spending they'd win,

But neglected to think of the

WHAT WOULD HAVE BEEN.

"The glazier's employment is the cobbler's loss."

"Yes, this is a detail o'er which you can't gloss."

The baker's real cost is the shoes he can't buy.

There's more to this story than

WHAT MEETS THE EYE.

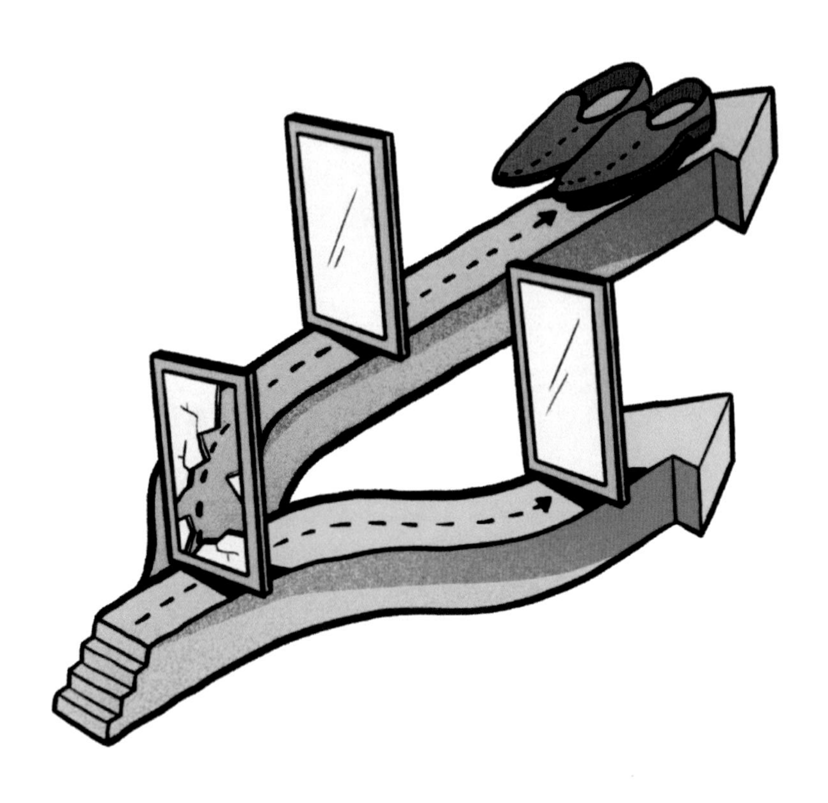

If breaking the window had not been Paul's aim,

the jobs and the spending would all be the same.

Destruction won't help. No, it's always bad news.
You'll see the new glass, but you won't see the shoes.
COUNTER
FACTUAL
MOVIE
THEATER
NOW SHOWING
BAKERY
GLASS REPAIR

Consider the seen, and the unseen as well.

You'll think much more clearly, as clear as a bell.

THE END

unless you are interested in...

The Non-Rhyming Explanation

A young boy throws a brick through the baker's window and a crowd gathers to consider the economic consequences of this event. They conclude (erroneously) that the broken window is good for the economy because it gives business to the glazier. This new spending can turn into more spending and employment because the glazier will spend the money on something. And whoever receives that money can now spend more, and so on. Therefore, the broken window is seen by the crowd as something that stimulates new spending and new employment.

The error in the crowd's thinking is that they have forgotten about what the baker would have done with the money if he did not use it to replace the broken window. He would have bought a new pair of shoes, which means that the broken window does not represent new spending and new employment. It only redirected the spending away from the cobbler and toward the glazier.

It is worse than just a redirection of spending, however. A window is broken – the little economy has lost real wealth. If we compare the two possible timelines, we see that in one the baker owns a new pair of shoes and an unbroken storefront window, but in the other he only owns a repaired storefront window.

This is the proper comparison. We should compare the outcome of some event or policy to the alternative timeline in which that event never happened or that policy was never put in place. We should not compare before and after only. This alternative timeline, the "what would have been," is called the **counterfactual**. Economics is all about counterfactuals because economics is all about choices. A choice is choosing one course of action over all others. The next-best course of action is the counterfactual (and the value of that next-best course of action is called the **opportunity cost** of the choice).

Therefore, this short story about a broken window teaches a lesson with broad applications. It applies to the destruction of natural disasters and war. Although Bastiat originally published this story in his 1850 essay, "That Which is Seen and That Which is Not Seen" in 1850, and Hazlitt popularized it in his 1946 book, **Economics in One Lesson**, the broken window fallacy is alive today. Journalists look for an optimistic take on hurricanes by saying that the increased spending on repairs and rebuilding is good for the economy. History textbooks still say that World War II brought the United States out of the Great Depression.

Hurricanes and wars are broken windows writ large, though. Journalists and history textbook authors (and many economists, unfortunately) ignore the counterfactual when they claim that these destructive events are beneficial. They do not see the computers, books, concert tickets, and fun vacations the hurricane victims would have bought. They do not see the cars, clothes, furniture, and food that producers in the United States could have made if the entire economy had not been mobilized for the war effort. Whatever may be said about the other outcomes of war, we cannot say that it is a boon for the economy.

The lesson also applies to government spending in general. We cannot ignore what taxpayers would have done with their own money if the government had not used it for doing the things that governments do. Governments cannot "stimulate the economy" because they can only redirect how money is used.

Moreover, taxes and inflation do not bring about new resources – they only increase the amount of our resources that are consumed according to politicians' and bureaucrats' preferences. Notably, government programs are not subject to the profit and loss test by which private businesses live and die, which means the best we can say about government programs is that we don't know how beneficial they are.

So let us learn from Bastiat and remember to consider the full picture. May we not stop at nice-sounding conclusions simply because they sound nice. We should learn how to use economics to analyze government policy and think critically about what journalists and government officials say. More often than not, there's more to their stories than what meets the eye.

ABOUT THE AUTHOR

Jonathan Newman is Assistant Professor of Economics and Finance at Bryan College and Associated Scholar of the Mises Institute. He earned his PhD in Economics at Auburn University. You can find his articles, lectures, and other work at mises.org.